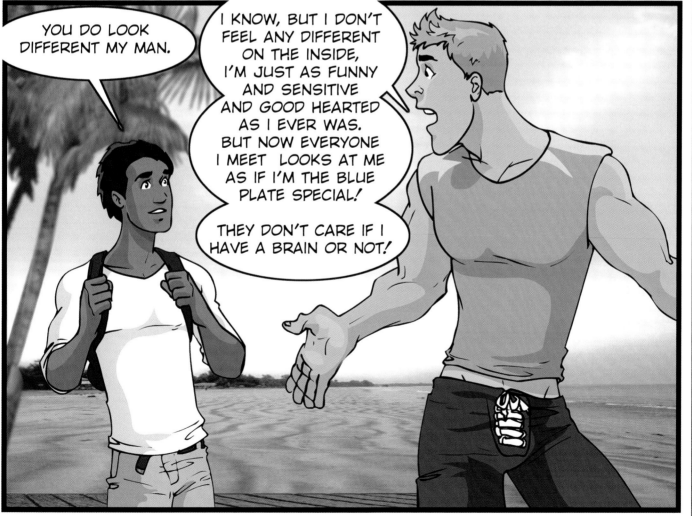

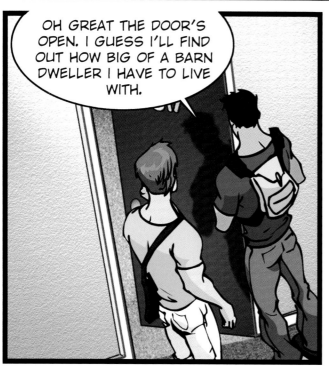

Special Thanks Nick Reedy and Wes Butler

Mid-Mall-Madness
by Joe Phillips

I DIDN'T KNOW WE WERE COMING TO THIS MALL WHEN YOU SAID THAT WE WERE GOING SHOPPING MOM!

WHAT DIFFERENCE DOES IT MAKE WHICH MALL WE SHOP AT?

FINDING CLOTHES THAT YOU WILL ACTUALLY WEAR IS HEARD ENOUGH...

THERE'S A STORE HERE WHERE I USED TO BUY ALL OF YOUR DAD'S BEST CLOTHES.

AWWW MOM! I DON'T WANT C MAN CLOTHES

NONSENSE HONEY, THIS IS A QUALITY STORE.

Abernathy&Finch

Abernathy&Finch

Abernathy&Finch

ex☆it!
BY JOE PHILLIPS
HEY ZED, I'M GLAD YOU CALLED. I WAS A LITTLE WORRIED ABOUT YOU AFTER YOUR BREAK-UP.
WELL I GUESS IT WAS ONE OF THOSE THINGS THAT WASN'T MEANT TO BE.
JoeBoy
maddison
VRROOOMM
BOYS R US
SOMEWHERE IN THE FUTURE...

LOCKER ROOM AFTER PRACTICE

WELL LOOK, IF IT ISN'T "THE FRESHMAN".

THERE'S NO BELL TO SAVE YOU NOW KID!

GIVE IT A REST GUYS, HOW MANY TIMES CAN I SAY I'M SORRY?

YEAH RIGHT, CRACK THE TEAMS CAPTAIN ON THE HEAD AND GET OFF SCOTT FREE... NOT!!!

SORRY IS NOT GONNA CUT IT!

WHAT ELSE CAN I DO?

WHATEVER I SAY...

KISS!

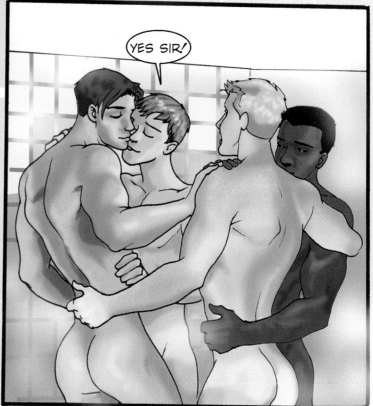

YES SIR!

SPECIAL THANKS TO RICH DI LEONARDO ART ASSIST AND PATRICK MULROY FOR "EDUMACATIN'" THE SCRIPT

...OUT?

SO GIVE ME A CALL AND WE'LL DO LUNCH OR SOMETHING.

DEFINATLY SOMETHING.

SORRY ABOUT THAT KAI, BUT HE WAS JUST SO CUTE!

IT'S ALL ABOUT FINE TUNING OF YOUR GAYDAR.

SEE THAT'S JUST WHAT I WAS TALKING ABOUT.

I CAN BARELY EVEN TELL WHO'S GAY THESE DAYS MORE LESS KNOW WHO TO AKS OUT.

GAYDAR?

YEAH, TAKE THAT "DAWSON" WANNABE OVER THERE. CUTE YES, BUT DEFINATLY STRAIGHT! WAY TOO OLD NAVY IF YOU KNOW WHAT I MEAN.

NOW THIS GUY IS AS GAY AS A THREE DOLLAR BILL.

THE DEEP WINE CHENILLE SWEATER IS A DEAD GIVE AWAY.

Straighten Up!

by Joe Phillips

¿69? BY JOE PHILLIPS

Boi4U: Dude you are so raw!

DangerBoy: I'll show you how raw I can be

Boi4U: Oh really? so what do you have in mind?

DangerBoy: Let's say it involves you and me in about every position you can think of.

Boi4U: I'm pretty imaginative

DangerBoy: and I'm double jointed!

Boi4U: Dude I'm there! Where the heck do you live?

DangerBoy: 619 6th ave. #9

619 6TH AVE. 20 MINUTES LATER...